Mister Got To Go

The Cat that wouldn't leave

Story by Lois Simmie

Illustrations by Cynthia Nugent

NORTHERN LIGHTS BOOKS FOR CHILDREN

Red Deer College Press

Northern Lights Books for Children are published by
Red Deer College Press
56 Avenue & 32 Street Box 5005
Red Deer Alberta Canada T4N 5H5

Acknowledgments
Edited for the Press by Tim Wynne-Jones.
Designed by Kunz + Associates.
Printed and bound in Canada by Friesens for Red Deer College Press.

Third Hardcover Printing 1998
First Paperback Printing 1996
Second Paperback Printing 1997
*Financial support provided by the Alberta Foundation for the Arts,
a beneficiary of the Lottery Fund of the Government of Alberta, and
by the Canada Council, the Department of Canadian Heritage and
Red Deer College.*

COMMITTED TO THE DEVELOPMENT OF CULTURE AND THE ARTS

Canadian Cataloguing in Publication Data
Simmie, Lois, 1932—
Mister got to go
(Northern lights books for children)
ISBN 0-88995-127-6 (bound) — ISBN 0-88995-157-8 (pbk.)
I. Nugent, Cynthia, 1954— II. Title. III. Series.
PS8587.I314M5 1995 jC813'.54 C94-910896-0
PZ7.S55Mi 1995

For Odette Simmie, Daniel Simmie and Christopher Simmie.
And for Oreo, Gatsby and Josie.
 —Lois Simmie

For Matt Petley-Jones, with thanks.
—Cynthia Nugent

One dark and rainy night at the edge
of a city on the edge of an ocean,
a stray cat came walking down
the beach.

   Across from an old hotel covered
with vines, the cat stopped. As he
looked at that place, he got a
strange, warm feeling inside him. I
think, thought the cat, I am tired of
being a stray cat.

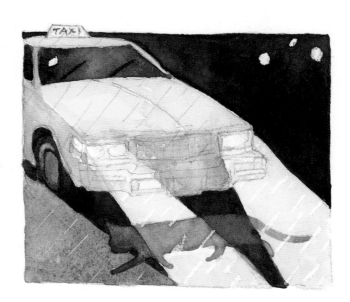

He trotted over, jumped up on a window ledge, and scratched on the window.

A man, whose name was Mr. Foster, looked up.

"My word," he said when he saw the cat. "You are a sorry, soggy sight." He opened the window and the cat stepped in. "You can stay until the rain stops," he said, shutting the window. "Then you've got to go." Mr. Foster was the hotel manager and was used to giving orders.

The cat sat down on the wide windowsill and began to lick the rain off his thick, gray fur. He was smiling all over inside himself, for he knew from the moment he stepped inside the Sylvia Hotel that he was a stray cat no longer.

Mr. Foster went back to the work on his desk, and the wind blew the rain at the window in big wet bunches. Through the door of Mr. Foster's office, the cat could see the cozy hotel lobby with its red striped chairs, soft lights, and gleaming old wood. With a very large sigh, the cat lay down on the windowsill and began to purr. He watched Mr. Foster till his eyes slowly closed and he slept.

"What a nice cat," said Miss Pritchett,

the night clerk, when she brought
Mr. Foster a cup of tea.

"Maybe he is and maybe he isn't,"
said Mr. Foster. "But whatever he is,
he's not staying long. As soon as it
stops raining, that cat's got to go."

And in the morning, when it stopped
raining, Mr. Foster put the cat out on
the sidewalk and shut the door.

A cold wind was blowing off the
ocean. The cat shivered and walked
around behind the hotel to see what
he could see. The back door was open,
so he slipped inside and sat in an open
elevator, where it was nice and warm.
He watched the people hurrying this
way and that. Outside, it was
raining again.

Up on the main floor, Mr. Foster pressed

the button for the service elevator. The door of the metal cage shut and up went the cat.

"You again?" said Mr. Foster when the elevator door opened. "We can't have a cat in the hotel, you know." He stepped in and pressed a button. "Oh no, we have no use for a cat here at the Sylvia. Absolutely none. As soon as it stops raining, you've got to go."

The cat looked like he was listening, but really he was thinking how pleased he was that his new home had this thing for riding up and down. He liked it a lot.

And so, every time Mr. Foster

put the cat out, the cat came back in
and rode up the elevator. He played
with the ball of wool at the end of
Miss Pritchett's knitting, and she gave
him tuna sandwiches from her lunch.
Old Harry, the bellhop, saved him
leftovers from the Room Service trays.
And the cook gave him scraps
from the kitchen.

"Now don't get too fond of that cat," Mr. Foster would say as he hurried past on some important errand. "Remember what I said. That cat's got to go."

Dogs were not allowed in the Sylvia Hotel.

One day when Mr. Foster was working at the front desk, a large lady in a bushy fur coat came in and asked for a room. As soon as he saw her, the cat arched his back and all his hair stood straight up.

"Behave yourself," said Mr. Foster under his breath. The cat hissed.

"Oh, I'm sorry, Madam. This is a stray cat who just came in out of the rain. I apologize for his bad manners."

The lady growled deep in her throat.

Mr. Foster was startled. He was a very polite man and expected other people to be polite, too.

"Well, I can understand your being upset," he said, trying to push away the cat, who had jumped onto the desk and was hissing at the lady.

"Grrrrr..." said the lady.

"My word," said Mr. Foster. "I don't think—"

The lady gave a yappy little bark. The cat spat at the lady. Suddenly, from between the buttons of her big fur coat, a black, furry nose and two bright eyes appeared. The little dog saw the cat and started barking like crazy. The cat flew off the desk and streaked for the windowsill in Mr. Foster's office.

When the lady with the big furry coat

and the small furry dog was gone, Mr. Foster looked at the cat and laughed.

"Well, Mister Cat, you are a good dog detector, I'll say that for you. But that doesn't mean you can stay. Oh my, no. We can't have a cat at the Sylvia Hotel. As soon as it stops raining..." He peered out the window. It was still raining. It rains all the time in Vancouver.

One day, a man came to take some pictures of the Sylvia Hotel. The cat was lying on a red striped chair in the lobby just as if he were in his own living room, which of course he was. He knew that.

"You can take a picture of that cat while you're at it," said Mr. Foster. "He is rather handsome, and since they're all so fond of him, it will give them something to remember him by when he's gone."

Mr. Foster had the photograph of the cat framed, and he hung it in the lobby himself.

The cat really was handsome.

He was much fatter than when he first came to the hotel, and his coat shone. After his picture was hung in the lobby, he became rather conceited.

There was a small bathroom

beside the manager's office, and one morning Mr. Foster noticed cat hair in his toothbrush that hung beside the sink. When the cat went into the bathroom, Mr. Foster crept up and peeked in. The cat was brushing his whiskers—first one side, then the other—against Mr. Foster's toothbrush.

"Cat whiskers!" cried Mr. Foster. "Cat whiskers," he grumbled as he hung a new toothbrush holder and toothbrush high up on the wall. "We can't have these sorts of goings-on here, absolutely not. This is a first-class hotel. That cat's got to go."

Rain drummed the window. Mr. Foster sighed. He left the old toothbrush where it was.

One rainy afternoon, a lady phoned

down from the third floor to say a raccoon was looking in her window. This upset Mr. Foster.

"Thieves!" he shouted, grabbing a broom and running to the service elevator. "Bandits!" he yelled, startling the cat, who was sitting in the elevator waiting for a ride down to the kitchen for his lunch. "Those blasted creatures climb up the vines to the third-floor ledge to steal the pigeon eggs. They're always scaring the wits out of our guests." Mr. Foster was so excited that he didn't notice the cat get off the elevator with him.

In Room 327, Mr. Foster threw open both windows

and leaned out, swatting at the raccoon with the broom. While Mr. Foster dangled from one window, the raccoon tumbled in the other window and the cat jumped on it.

There was a terrible uproar as the cat chased

the raccoon and the raccoon chased the cat. Around and around, along the ledge and through the room they went, in one window and out the other and back again.

Fur flew. The lady screamed and jumped up and down on the bed. Old Harry and Miss Pritchett came running.

Mr. Foster yelled and waved the broom, hitting everything but the raccoon and cat. Suddenly, they slipped off the ledge and fell, hissing and spitting, down three stories to the ground. The raccoon streaked for the park.

Mr. Foster leaned out the window and looked down

at the cat. He was just sitting down there in the rain. Mr. Foster closed his eyes. He had a headache.

Mr. Foster drove the cat to the cat doctor,

who stitched him up in so many places he looked like a patchwork cat.

"What is this cat's name?" the doctor asked. She needed it for her report.

"Oh, my word. His name?" asked Mr. Foster. "Well, he doesn't really have a name. You see, we keep saying he's got to go...."

Beside the word *Name* on the report, the cat doctor wrote *Got To Go*.

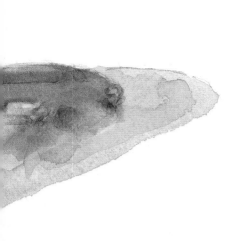

CLINIC REPORT
NAME _Mr. Got to Go_
DESCRIPTION _altercation with raccoon resulting in defenestration._
TREATMENT _general stitching, swabbing, daubing, bandaging, plastering, patting, and soothing._
PROGNOSIS _excellent_
SIGNED _Dr. Susan_

They drove back to the hotel in the rain.

The windshield wipers seemed to be saying *Got to... Go... Got to... Go....* Mr. Foster looked at the cat. It looked like he was smiling.

It's seven years since that dark and rainy night the stray cat came walking down the beach to the Sylvia Hotel. Every so often, Mr. Foster says, "My word, is that cat still here? He's got to go, you know. As soon as it stops raining, that cat's got to go."

Sometimes the sun is shining when he says it.